VENI, VIDI, VICI

VENI, VIDI, VICI

I Came, I Saw, I Conquered

PAM JACKSON

VENI, VIDI, VICI
I CAME, I SAW, I CONQUERED

iUniverse books may be ordered through booksellers or by contacting:

iUniverse
1663 Liberty Drive
Bloomington, IN 47403
www.iuniverse.com
1-800-Authors (1-800-288-4677)

ISBN: 978-1-4917-5605-8 (sc)
ISBN: 978-1-4917-5607-2 (e)

Library of Congress Control Number: 2014922796

Print information available on the last page.

iUniverse rev. date: 11/23/2015

To my dog Charley, the star of *Travels with Charley*, who went to doggie heaven in 2008. He was the greatest dog of all the great dogs we've had, even though all our dogs are special. But Charley knew my heart and soul. He would just give me a look. His collar still remains in my car right next to me and always will.

Preface

Veni came into my life two years ago, and with her, I've experienced a series of adventures that I have not gone through with any of our other dogs.

A professional dog trainer for the past thirty years, I have placed my passion into trying to understand how dogs think. In the past two years, I started putting my perceived thoughts of my new dog Veni to paper in the form of short stories by Veni from the perspective of Veni. Veni the dog is the author of her stories, and I am her ghostwriter.

We picked up Veni as a new puppy in Italy via Hungary in November 2012. She is a Pumi, a rare herding breed, from Hungary. I met Veni's sire, one of the top champion Pumik in Europe at the World Dog Show in Paris. Veni's mother is a show dog and sheepherder. She has been writing from the very first day we met. She is very comical and has been quite the challenge, even for a person who has been training dogs as long as I have.

Veni writes her stories about her housemates (both animal and human), her travels and dog shows, and the funny things she observes in the world. From time to time, she receives letters in response to her stories from other dog friends.

Acknowledgments

First and foremost, I want to thank my husband for encouraging me to do Veni's letters. Her letters put a smile on his face and laughter in his heart. And I have to thank all my other friends, mostly Dave, Hoover's dad and Veni's biggest fan.

Prologue

I was born on September 10, 2012, in Hungary. I am a Pumi, a Hungarian herding breed. Even though we fought, I loved all my brothers and sisters. When I was about six weeks old, I found out that I had been sold to some people in America. If human babies are sold, the seller goes to jail. And if a mom has four or five babies at one time, she keeps them because she loves them. I do not think it is fair that my human mom sold me. I wanted to stay with her and my brothers and sisters. I wanted to herd sheep in Hungary, like my dog mom. I met my new parents from America in Venice, Italy. They named me Venice, but they call me Veni.

This is my adventure.

Letter 1

I first met my new mom and dad in Florence, Italy, in November 2012. My real human mom, who lives in Hungary, sent me away to a new home. How could she? Did she not like me? She met my aunt Aurora, the owner of my dog dad, somewhere between Italy and Hungary to give me away to some people who live in the United States. She wanted me as far away from her as possible. Aunt Aurora took me to her house to meet my dog dad. She had several Pumik besides my dad. He was very handsome, and I think he liked me, but I was so scared. She kept me for a week, and I fell in love with my auntie.

Then my auntie put me in a car and drove me from Venice to Florence to meet my new parents. I did not want to go. I love my dad and my auntie, and I missed my real mom. I was crying.

I met my new human mom and dad at a restaurant in Florence the same night. They were strangers. I only speak Hungarian. How can I understand these strange people? I hid behind my aunt Aurora. I wanted to stay with her. Why, oh why, do I have to go to the USA?

That same night, I had to spend the night with my new parents. This is when I found out that my new mom trains dogs for a living. And I was afraid of my new human dad. All bad news.

The next day, Auntie met us at the airport. She threw a ball for me, and I took it right back to her. She was fun. Then she handed me to my new mom to board a plane for Paris. My new mom carried me, but I kept looking back at Auntie with tears in my eyes. Nobody I loved wanted me.

We arrived in Paris, and we had to run to catch our second plane to the United States. My mom put me on the floor with a pee pad so I did not have to hold it for thirteen hours. She got in bad trouble when she was caught. We almost missed our plane.

I was such a good girl on the airplane, only because I had lots of time to think and cry. I held my pee for nine hours. Then I just could not help it. I whined. I learned how to do this well. My mom took me out of the crate, and Dad cleaned me up and then put me back in. Mom tried to sneak me into the bathroom with a pee pad but got caught and was sent back to her seat. I learned that my new mom does not follow the rules.

We arrived at my new home in Chualar, California. It is in the country with horses, cows, rabbits, roadrunners, and snakes. I met Levi, another Pumi. Dad held me outside in his lap. Levi came running out very quickly toward me. He frightened me so much that I snapped at him. I then met the standard poodle, Demi. She hated me at first sight.

So far, all is not well at my new home. Why did they send me away? Boo hoo.

Veni

Letter 2

Hi, Auntie,

I got in trouble twice in the last two days. I got on top of a little table in between their two chairs in the sitting room. Mom found me with a fake peach in my mouth. She scolded me and put it back. As soon as her back was turned, she caught me standing on the table again, trying to get the same peach. I liked it. I also learned to get on another table in the family room. It is very small, so it was quite a chore to balance on it, but I managed. Mom got on me, but I heard her telling Dad about it, and they were laughing. I know I am cute.

Demi still ignores me. I think she is jealous because I am young and beautiful. She is beautiful too, but I can see some gray on her muzzle. She needs to go to the beauty shop. She is a champion, and I am not, so her nose is in the air much of the time. She sleeps on top of the couch like a cat, and Levi and I rest on the part of the couch where normal people sit. We are regular dogs. Oh well. I guess we have to put up with her. Maybe someday she will like me. Who wouldn't?

I am on my second week of dog training. Yuck! My mom thinks I am doing well though. After all, my dog dad is smart, and my dog mom is a real working dog that herds sheep. My mom wants me to learn how to do this also, along with freestyle dancing, obedience, competition, and on and on and on. She wants to keep my busy all the time. I do not know when I will ever have time to rest. Ugh!

Love and kisses,

Veni

Letter 3

Love to you, Aunt Aurora,
I have been in the United States for almost a month now.
It has been a rough week, so I haven't had time to write.
My mom has been training several dogs, and I have been
trying to train Levi and Demi. And Mom has been trying
to train me.

I found a real treasure, a ball, underneath an old corner cupboard in the sitting room. I worked and worked on it, trying to get it out with my paws. I crawled under the cupboard, and finally, after about ten minutes, I got it out.

And you know what? Levi watched me, tapping his toenail and staring at me, and as soon as I got it out, he took it. He jumped on Mom and Dad's bed, knowing I could not jump up that far, and chewed on it with a real gleam in his eyes as he stared at me. Then he dropped it on the floor to share it with me, or so I thought. And just as I was ready to grab it, he jumped down and got it before I did. He then jumped up on the bed and teased me like this for the next hour. He never let me have the ball. Mom needs to ground him. He does not know how to share.

Demi is coming around a little bit. She still has her nose in the air, but she will sometimes play with me. But when she plays, it is very serious play. It is almost like she would like to hurt me. I do not know what I have done to her to make her dislike me so much, except the fact that I am not a poodle.

I mentioned the old corner cupboard in Mom and Dad's room. Between you and me, Aunt Aurora, I am a little worried about the home you found for me. All the furniture in Mom's home is old. I kind of think that they are poor, so I am not sure how long they will be able to afford to buy my food. This is all I think about. I have to have my food. Are you sure that Aramis is my only sire? My mom says I eat like and chew like a Lab. I will keep you informed. I may have to go back to Italy to have some good food at your mother's house.

I had a bad day of training this week. I just did not want to do it. I threw a fit, but Mom made me do it. I gave in. Why did you send me a to a dog trainer's home? I love her, but she makes me behave. I would really like to do what I want to do.

Have a great Christmas and happy New Year. My mom's house is all decorated for Christmas, but I am not allowed in to see the tree. She does not trust me. Can you believe it? I did chew another phone cord. Dad had to replace it. I am sorry, but it was fun until I got caught.

Love and kisses,

Veni

Letter 4

Dear Aunt Aurora, I am sorry I have not written, but I have been so busy. I had to help my mom make Christmas cookies, and then she would not even give me one. She said they are not suitable for dogs. My mother is kind of a health food nut. My treats are dried sweet potatoes, for heaven's sake. Doesn't she know that I like meat? I am a dog after all. My dad sneaks me some treats when Mom is not looking.

But guess what? They have an apple tree in the backyard, and the apples fall on the ground. Yes! I run out and eat them as quickly as I can until Mom catches me. She runs after me, and I run from her. She is so afraid that I will get the green apple two-step, whatever that means. I am still learning English.

I am the very first dog that Mom and Dad have ever had that will eat apples off the apple tree, run on the high hedges, dig in the large flower pots, eat dried peaches, and chew on everything. I love their rugs and pillows. Pillows should not have tassels. They look much better without them.

My mom heard me chewing on something very crunchy in their family room when she was in the kitchen. I was chewing on one of their old boxes. As far as I am concerned, they need to get rid of all those old things anyway and get new. But she says they are Early American, and some are over a hundred years old. I told you that I am worried that they could not afford me. Are they old too?

Well, let's talk about Demi. She nipped me a couple of days ago. I just got on the couch where she was perched on her usual place where a queen would sit. I screamed. Mom ran in and yelled at Demi. I barked at her. Mom told me that female dogs are called "bitches." I looked it up in the dictionary, and Demi's picture was right next to the word. She is jealous of me. She used to play with Levi, but Levi likes me better. Who wouldn't? I am adorable.

This is my first Christmas. I am going to meet my two human brothers. Chris, the oldest, is an attorney. Shawn, my youngest brother, is a produce broker like my dad. I met Shawn, and I like him very much. I met Chris just briefly when we all went out to dinner. We three dogs had to stay in the car. How rude! I do have to talk to Chris about my share of the estate. He may not like that. I doubt there is anything, but just in case.

My brothers both live in a beautiful place called

Pebble Beach. They are close to the ocean. I have to live in the country with all those smelly horses, cows, rabbits, deer, raccoons, and, during the summer, snakes. Chris has two children, nine-year-old Nicholas and four-year-old Ava. Shawn's children are five-year-old Avery and three-year-old Gage.

I met Nicholas after dinner. Mom took me out of my crate, and Nicholas held me. He said he not only loved me but he loved me so much. I was pretending to be sweet and good. I hope I can keep up the act for a while longer.

I will write again after I meet everyone on Christmas Day. I am staying home with Dad today on Christmas Eve. He is sick with a cold and offered to keep me home. Mom is going to Chris' house. Poor Dad. I will try to be good, but I doubt I can do it for very long. Will five minutes do?

Love and kisses,

Veni

PS: Is my English getting better? Hungarian is much easier. Oh, I forgot to tell you something. I learned something new today. I went out to go potty, finished my job, and then scraped the grass really hard with my back feet, like boy dogs do. Levi just stared at me. Mom was in shock. I am trying to teach Levi, who has never done this, to be a real man.

Letter 5

Dear Aunt Aurora,

I will send you photos soon. Some were taken on Christmas Day. I had a great time. All the kids love me. I was on my best behavior. It is so difficult to be good. I had to wait until I got home to start barking, digging, and chewing. I had a couple of accidents when I got home also. My mom was not happy. But after all, I am still a little puppy. I met an old gentlemen Lab named Striker at Shawn's house. He came on a little strong for me at first, so I had to put him in his place.

His owner is a dog judge. I could feel her eyes on me all the time. She was judging me. She kept looking to see if I had reach and drive. I had no idea what she was talking about. I did reach very far to put my paw on Striker's head. I learned to really like him. And it was discussed if I would have to help Mom drive home. She is not a good night driver, and Dad had to stay home because he was still not well.

The dog judge told me that it had nothing to do with my reaching Striker and driving Mom home. It was about my movement. Am I a show dog? She kept saying that she really liked me. I knew I was special.

Dad wanted Mom to put me on their bed before I had to go to sleep in my crate. Demi would not allow it. As I was lying in my crate thinking, it finally hit me. She is jealous of me because she is really in love with Levi. They are not really brother and sister, but boyfriend and girlfriend. No wonder she hates me. She is tall and willowy with a beautiful face, except for the gray. I am young, beautiful, and petite with lots more personality. Levi now prefers me. I think that Mom needs to find Demi a good psychologist. She may have to go on antidepressants.

You know what else she does? When Levi and I are wrestling, she bites Levi's back legs and barks. She wants him all to herself. She needs help.

Love and kisses,
Veni
December 2012

Letter 6

Dear Auntie,

I was left alone in my crate for four hours tonight. I think I need to call Animal Control. Mom and Dad went out to dinner with friends, and they left me alone for the first time with Demi and Levi. I hated it. They fed me way too early, three thirty specifically. They thought it was time for me to get used to being alone. They usually get me a dog sitter.

I told you that they are poor. I was right. They did not want to pay for a dog sitter for me. I was a good girl because I did not wet my crate. As soon as they got home, they let us all out to go potty. Whew! I was crossing my little legs, but I made it. Mom gave us all a treat. Guess what it was? Dried sweet potatoes. I was so hungry, but come on. Where's the beef?

I have another complaint. They take away my water at six o'clock in the evening. They think I drink too much water. Huh. So one night, I was so thirsty that I found a way to get through the gate that separates the two yards. I have two yards. One is where the pool is; one is from Mom and Dad's bedroom. So, I found a way to get through the fence that separates the two yards. I had to squeeze my body to make it small. It was a little difficult because I love to eat.

When Mom let us back in a few minutes later, she noticed I was soaking wet. She yelled at poor Dad to get some towels. I needed some water. The pool is full of water, but as I leaned over, I guess I fell in. I am a good swimmer though. I got myself out right away. Mom is calling a handyman to fix the problem. Well, this is the news for the day. Demi has not been to the doctor yet.

Love to all. Tell my dad hello for me.

Veni

Letter 7

Dear Aunt Aurora,

I just had to tell you about my very bad day. I should have stayed in bed all day long. It started out with my training lesson. My mom described me as a little monster. I just did not feel like doing anything that she wanted me to do. I wanted to play with Levi. Can't I even have a day off, for heaven's sake? We stayed outside until I did what she wanted me to do. I could see perspiration on her forehead. She would not give in. Again, Aunt Aurora, why did you send me to a dog trainer?

Then Mom had to pick up her car from Monterey. Her stepmother, who lives in Mom and Dad's guest house, offered to take her. I went along with them. I had only met her stepmother once. Mom drove her car because she is such a slow driver, which meant I had to sit in her lap. She said it was okay just so I did not pee on her. Well, she said pee, so I did. She was not happy. She had a big spot on her pants. Well, I know that, when Mom tells me to pee, I do. So I did. It isn't my fault. Mom tried to put me in the backseat with her stepmother's dog, Maggie.

I sat as far as I could from her, but she snapped at me twice. I really do not like little, white, pudgy dogs now. But why did she not like me? I am so likable. I think it is because she is fat.

Just because my training session did not go well in the morning, Mom took me out when I got home. Hadn't I been through enough in one day? I was too tired to fight her, so I just gave in.

Love,
Veni

PS: I am finally getting used to Dad. He gives me treats and lets me bite him on the leg all the time. He knows I am a herding breed and I need to do this. And he does not make me do anything. He just might become my favorite.

Letter 8

Dear Hoover,

I thought I should tell you a little story. All dogs know that poodles are in the top ten smartest dogs, right? Well, this might be a misnomer. Notice my new word. Mom makes me study the dictionary.

I told you that I love apples from the apple tree. Mom has to go out every day to pick them up so I will not eat them. I try to beat her out there, but she always catches me. Demi was looking through the ivy in the backyard, sniffing and jumping up to look inside. I watched her, and as soon as she left, I ran over to see what was so interesting. My mom saw me. She could only see my rear end because I was so far into the ivy. I found it. I put it in my mouth and ran. Demi and even Levi, who I thought was smart, started chasing me.

They thought I found something special. I let them run and run and run after me. Mom could not catch me either, so she opened the back door, and I ran in the house with Demi and Levi behind me. It was the most beautiful green apple I have ever seen. Apples are so sweet and tasty. I am the only dog that truly appreciates high-end hors d'oeuvres. I let them think it was a ball. Ha! Hoover, I know how you feel about poodles, so I thought you would enjoy my poodle story.

Love,
Veni

PS: Mom bought me a new training collar today. I was really excited until she put it on me. Why? I am such a good girl. She took me out to do my sit, stay, and down-stay, and guess what? I was so perfect that she did not even use the collar. Does she think I am a stupid girl? I knew right away that I had better do what she wanted. I even went down before she told me. My downs are really good, Hoover.

Letter 9

Dear Hoover,

I am a bird dog. Dad let me out in the backyard to go potty, and Mom asked him to pick up the apples. Thank goodness he does not see as well as Mom because he missed one. I was so happy. I picked it up, and I was holding it in my mouth when I noticed some birds. I was transfixed, my newest word. They were flying, flapping their wings, and walking on the ground. I stood so still with the apple in my mouth with my tail straight out. My tail is supposed to be over my back, and I held my right leg up. I was pointing. Am I a pointer, Lab, or Pumi? I am confused.

This morning at four o'clock, I cleaned Mom's eyes and ears. I then worked on Levi. His eyes were in a bad way. I worked on them for at least fifteen minutes. Then I cleaned out his ears. I like everyone clean at my house. They need to start taking care of themselves soon. I do not have the time to take care of their hygiene forever, for heaven's sake.

Love,
Veni

PS: Levi told me that my deceased brother was a stage star. I had an actor in my family. I will write in detail soon.

As seen in the Monterey Herald

Letter 10

Dear Auntie,

Mom started back to work this week. Guess what? I like it. I met two very handsome boy dogs. She trains girl dogs as well, but I prefer boys. I met a little, short dog named Toby. He likes me, and I like him. He lives in Pebble Beach, right by the ocean. I get to see him every week for a while. Maybe I could live with one of my brothers so I could see him more often.

Speaking of brothers, my oldest brother, Chris, the attorney, talked to me about my share of the estate. He did not want to offer me hardly anything. It was not fair. After all, all I want are my favorite toys and that little old box that is a hundred years old. It is very crunchy, and I really love it. He said that I cannot have the box and I have to share the toys with Levi and Demi. He is not my favorite brother.

I also met my pen pal, Hoover, a handsome Lab that my mom trained. Wow! He likes me too. He is a tall dog. Do I want the short dog, the tall dog, or maybe the old gentlemen dog, Striker? This is a difficult choice. There will be more boy dogs in the future. I will just take my time. After all, I am young and beautiful.

Speaking of beautiful, Mom did get Demi in to the

doggie psychiatrist. She is on meds, and she has been so much nicer to me. She still looks at herself in the mirror a lot, and she has her nose in the air. Just wait until I am a champion! But she is tolerating me a little better. She is still jealous when I play with Levi, but at least she is not trying to kill me like she did before. Whew!

Guess what I found in the backyard? A cigar. Mom was very upset because she said that dogs should not smoke. It probably came from Dad's bar, dedicated to the famous Charley, my actor brother. I was just saving the cigar for one of my many doggie boyfriends. She took it away from me. Sorry, Toby, Hoover, and Striker. I will try again when she has her back turned.

Love,
Veni

Letter 11

Hi, Veni,

I enjoyed meeting you too. I think you should pick me. Yes, I am tall and handsome, but the fact that I am smart and a Lab should be enough. I know you are part Lab. We could get in a lot of trouble together. I could even teach you how to outfox your mom. She is a wonderful trainer, but you need to learn that you are the boss. The next time I see you, I will bring you an apple.

Hoover

Dear Hoover,

Oh, I like this. Bribery is good. I love apples, but can you afford me, Hoover? I was just looking at a diamond collar, and I know that Mom and Dad cannot afford it. There is a real problem with them. It is about my food. I will write later.

Love,
Veni

Veni,

Diamonds are for poodles. If we are going to hunt rats, swim, and play in the ivy, we don't even want to wear those stupid collars like your mom bought you. Think about it, girl.

Hoover

Dear Hoover,

You sure are a smooth talker, Hoover. I have to give you points for this, but if I saw a rat, I would run the other way. I am a girl after all, and remember one thing. Diamonds are a girl's best friend.

Veni

Dear Veni,

If diamonds are a girl's best friend, why did your mom come home from Italy with you instead of a diamond?

Hoover

Hoover,

Oh my, oh my, oh my, Hoover! What happened to your silver tongue? I am a diamond. A diamond in the ruff perhaps, but a diamond of the highest quality. I have been studying. I did notice a permanent scar on your muzzle when we met. Was this from a girl dog that you angered with that silver tongue of yours? Huh? Grrrr.

Veni

Hi, Veni,

I hope you enjoyed our meeting today as much as I did. You are growing into a beautiful young lady. Hoover doesn't understand that a young lady just naturally loves diamonds. Actually, your eyes remind me of two sparkling diamonds. I forgot to tell you that my mom bought me some of your sweet potato treats. They are delicious. Also, she was making a wonderful apple cake this evening and gave me a bite of the apple. I knew you loved them, so they certainly must be great.

I'm looking forward to seeing you next week. I promise to work on the down command so you will be proud of me.

XO,
Toby

Thank you, Toby. You certainly are a smooth talker.

Love,
Veni

Dear Hoover,
Why have I not heard from you?

Veni,
Well, Veni. You have not heard from me because I was in the hospital. The other day when I was on the beach, I saw a surfer being attacked by a shark. I swam out, scared off the shark, and pulled the surfer to shore. I will probably have another scar so you will probably not want to see me again.

Hoover

Hi, Veni,

Hi, I am Hoover's brother, Chip, the Christmas pup my dad's parents gave to their granddaughters. I am watching my mom cook, but I would rather be watching you. I don't have scars like my brother Hoover. I am younger, but I like older women. You could come to Colorado, or I could come to California. Tell your mom I am on a ten-minute sit stay, and I don't even have a trainer.

Chip

Dear Chip,

You sure are handsome. I do like chocolate, so I would really like to meet you. It would be really nice if you could bring a box of chocolates. A little diamond might be nice too. I love diamonds and younger men. Woo hoo.

Love,
Veni

Dear Willow,
What do you think I should do? I need advice.

Veni,
Chip looks good, Veni. I also had to endure the football thing. But I am a pro at this. I get treats when Mom goes outside to cuss. I can hardly wait for the Super Bowl. More treats! I have to be in a show the day before, even though I am only five months old. I am sure to get treats there, as this is the only way I will walk on a lead. I hope you dump Hoover and hook up with Chip.

Your friend,
Willow

Hi, Veni,
You must come to Colorado. Guess what my mom was cooking? Spaghetti. It was way better than chocolate, and for dessert, she made apple pie, fresh from my very own tree. My mom thinks I should be able to eat whatever I like. I even had a little Italian wine. You will not be homesick ever again. Come visit.

Chip

Dear Chip,
This really sounds good, but as I mentioned before, I think that my mom and dad are poor. I know they could not afford to fly me to Colorado. Is this in Italy? After all, they cut out one of my meals, and I am so weak. This is one of the reasons I have to lie in their chairs and chew. I have to eat something. They are so mad at me right now. If they would feed me more, I would not eat chairs. The apple tree

is bare now, so I do not even have a snack. Dad has a wine cellar. Maybe I should try some?

Love,
Veni

Dear Veni,
My parents are rich. My dad is a mortgage broker, and my mom is an engineer. I will send you a one-way ticket. I have a great idea. I will get the ticket for February 3, Super Bowl Sunday. Your parents will be so involved in the game that they will never miss you. I can have my brother pick you up and take you to the airport. I will pick you up at the Denver airport. My dad and I are big Niner fans, but I would give up the game for you, unlike your parents who ignore you during the games.

Love,
Chip

Oh, Chip. You do take after your brother Hoover. He is older, and you are younger, but you are both very smooth talkers. I have to run this by my brother Levi and my other doggie friends. Toby is out of the equation. He is just too short for me. He has offered to be my financial advisor. You will hear from me soon.

Veni

Veni, *foos*. This means "pay attention" and "heel" in German. Do I have your attention? I always hear my parents telling that to my sister who is a very brave German shepherd. She is in Schutzhund training. My peeps speak German to her all the time, and now I have decided I should learn my native language too. Perhaps you can learn it with me. You see, I am a Pomeranian and German, and I love to meet new pups, especially beautiful ladies. I think you need a little international flavor to remind you of home.

I am named after a Marine, and I have the heart of a warrior just like my dad. I was only 2.4 ounces when I was born, but now I am two and a half pounds of all man.

I have many diamond collars here at my house that my Pom mom never wore because my people say they pull out your coat. A curly-haired girl like you would look beautiful in them. Remember, estate jewelry passed down through the generations is the best kind.

Luv,
Gunny, your Pomeranian friend

Dear Gunny,

I would love to meet you also. I love men in uniform and appreciate your service to our country. I am from Hungary but am now a citizen of the United States. Hoover did fight in Afghanistan, so I do have to give him some consideration. But he has not mentioned diamonds, whereas you have. I am a little overweight though. I would have to get on a strict diet to get down to two and a half pounds. I weigh fifteen. Mom and Dad have cut out one of my meals already, and I am starving, but I will try. I cannot promise, however, because food is all I think about. I do love estate jewelry though.

Love and kisses,
Veni

Letter 12

Dear Auntie Aurora,

I am turning gray. My body is black, but my muzzle is gray. And I am gray around my eyes. Do I have some kind of disease? I look like Demi, my biggest fear, and she is old. I just looked in the mirror, and I jumped back. This cannot be. I am just four months old. I need to go to the beauty shop right away. And Demi is going to have to share her meds. I have many boy dog friends who are not going to like this new look. Am I supposed to be gray like Levi? Please tell me no.

Love,
Veni

PS: I have put on weight also. I weigh fifteen pounds. I am going to start doing Zumba and kickboxing aerobics with Mom. Everything at once. This is too much.

Letter 13

To my dear friends,

And guess what? I found out why I am turning gray. I was sound asleep last night when I heard a noise. Demi was standing over me with a spray can in her paw. Gray paint. I caught her. She looked at me, raised her eyebrow, showed her teeth, turned, and walked away with her tail straight up. Just like a show horse. I need to get her some sleeping pills and increase her antidepressants.

Veni

Letter 14

Dear Lady-in-Waiting,

Yes, the parental units are armed and dangerous. They work around felons all day and feel compelled to protect us 24/7. I hear them tell prison stories all the time, and I think that is what made them so mean to my brother and me. They feel we should tough it out and work through our lunch-less days. You can feel my ribs, Veni. All of them. My brother Gunny is so skinny that I can knock him over with one swat. I think we all need sustenance quickly. How do your mom's old boxes taste?

My mom doesn't think a fat dog will win at the show, but I disagree. Girls like love handles, right, Veni? If you decide to come visit, you may not recognize me. I got a big boy show cut last night, and my crazy mom trimmed me with thinning shears for three hours. I look like a topiary. That woman needs a hobby. How can anyone spend so much time torturing a puppy? I know you are in the same situation I am, so maybe we should eliminate the moms in our lives. I hear dads don't wash or trim dogs. I know our dads would feed us more too.

We could be dangerous together, Veni, and I am a bad boy. Mom says that to me all the time.

In lockdown and feeling lonely,
Chesty, your Pomeranian friend

Letter 15

Hi, Auntie Aurora,

My mom's first dog student canceled because it is so cold, so I had a minute to write. I knew this was going to happen. It was just a matter of time. My mom's good friend, the dog judge, was talking to Mom about the economy. I have to look this up in the dictionary. I noticed that Mom was feeding me my noon feeding. She told Mom that she should cut out that feeding and I should be fed just two times a day. I am going to starve. What do I get at noon? A dried sweet potato. The apples on the apple tree are just about gone. I am so hungry. I knew that there was trouble in this household. Mom and Dad have to work a little harder to be able to afford me.

Maybe you could send me a plane ticket to Italy. I promise I will be a good girl. I am getting into so much trouble that I think I need a vacation. Could I have some pasta when I get there? I have been working on my house. I am a very busy girl. I chewed a hole in the rug, gnawed on Mom's chair and Dad's, and finished off all the tassels on the pillows. Mom watches me, but I am really fast. She caught me yesterday and yelled. Can you believe it? I hid under the bed. She has a loud voice. I noticed that Demi had a big smile on her face. The meds are helping, but her picture is still under the word "bitch."

I have met some boy dogs here in the United States. All are handsome. But I want diamonds, and I am having a little trouble. They are not sure that diamonds would look good on me. But they will. I have heard that Italian boy dogs are very good looking. I will wait to hear from you. A ticket to Italy would be greatly appreciated.

Love and kisses,

Veni

PS: I am still beautiful. She said I am going through the uglies. I think this is unfair. Ticket, please.

Letter 16

Hi again, Auntie,

I just wanted to let you know that you will probably not hear from me for a week or two. I am going to be very busy. My mom and I will be babysitting Avery and Gage. Their mom has to go to the hospital. I think this will feel better. My job is to take care of three-year-old Gage. He likes to play with trucks and cars all day long. I have to learn how to push them for him with my paw. Mom will take care of five-year-old Avery. She loves jewelry and girly things. She also loves diamonds. Please note, Hoover and

Chip. She also goes to kindergarten. I wish I could go with her. I could play with all the toys and eat snacks. It is exhausting pushing trucks around all day long. Ugh. They are cute kids though. Perhaps not as cute as me, but cute nonetheless.

Over the weekend, Mom and Dad had to help their nephew decorate his house. There again, they could not afford a dog sitter, so we three had to go. We sat in the car for hours and hours. Then we had to travel to Santa Cruz for another forty-five minutes while they shopped and shopped and shopped. Finally at dinnertime, they stopped. We drove to a restaurant while they ate. My stomach was growling. It was way past my dinnertime. Then Dad walked out to the car with the most delicious hamburger patties. Levi and I ate so quickly. And Demi? She had to be hand-fed. We tried to get her food, but Dad told us to back up.

The very next day, we had to go back to finish the job. They kept talking about how great it looked, but they did not even offer to show us. The story of my life, Auntie. I am still waiting for my ticket to Italy. I have not heard a word. After babysitting, I will really need a vacation.

Love and kisses,
Veni

Letter 17

Veni, good Lord, I have been listening to you whine and whine, so please get over it. Your mother and father have a lot on their minds right now. They are very poor, and my mom is looking for a sister for me so she can hire your mom to help make her behave so I won't have to bark or bite her. That way, perhaps your mom will have some money to buy you those diamonds you so desperately want since your boyfriend seems so cheap. My mom says I am beyond training, but then what do you expect when you come from a very abused situation like I did? Gosh, I pee on the rug as soon as I hear a spark crackle from her fireplace. And those coyotes howling scare me to death. I don't think your mother is good enough to train me to forget. You be good and help push those trucks and cars all day long if you have to. I can't wait to have Mom tell me how you are doing while your big sister Tori recuperates.

Cracky

I think I am a mixed breed shorthair pointer

Letter 18a

Hi, Cracky,

Okay, good. I hope that your mom finds another dog. My mom does need the money. Sorry, but I have to tell the truth. My mom did say that I am the worst whiner she has ever seen. She says I talk too much also. I forgot to tell you my latest feat. I can hold a ball in my mouth while I pee, something I bet many dogs can do, but I can do something that I bet most dogs cannot do. I can pee and bark with a ball in my mouth. It is not easy, but I found out that it could be done.

Love,
Veni

PS: Thanks for the kind words, Cracky ... or Cranky?

Letter 18b

Hi, everyone,

I do not know. All these small dogs. Toby has decided to be my financial advisor, so I am thinking that Gunny should be my bodyguard. After all, he has had guard dog experience. Plus, his dad might have a gun. But we must not tell the president of the United States.

Veni

Letter 19

Dearest Veni,

Yes, in fact, I am an enlisted man, and I am far more fun than my brother is. He acts so dignified. You know how those officers are. I am all man even though I am only about six inches high at the withers. I heard you don't like short men, but I can use my sister to boost me up. I could even use my dad. He is a giant. I didn't know people could be so huge. My dad is six feet four inches tall. I know this is the reason he calls me his "little man." Anyone would be little compared to him.

Mom signed me up for my first dog show yesterday, and I have been practicing really hard to impress you. I have a lot of pizzazz, and I am perfect for the show world, according to Mom. When will your show career be starting? In preparation for my debut, Mom gave me a mani and pedi the other day. Let me tell you, boy. Did that hurt, Veni! I think I deserve a Purple Heart for my war injuries. I started screaming before she even touched me, just to let her know how much it might hurt. Then she snipped, and my toes turned into a river of blood. Then she told me to stop fussing, and she put this awful stinging stuff on them. It was so bad, Veni.

I know there must be a medal for bravery just for this.

I am not supposed to have pretty feet like Mom wants. I am a boy. I need my nails for digging.

These people just don't understand. I hear Mom talking about giving me another bath and trim before the show too. My future is looking very bleak if I have to stay here much longer. Veni, write soon. Your letters are the only thing that makes this prison life bearable.

Kisses,

Gunny

Letter 20

Gunny,

Oh no. Maybe I do not want to be a show dog. I was not aware that this was the plan in the first place. I may have to refuse to get out of the car at dog shows, like Levi does. My nails hurt just thinking about it. Levi would grab his leash as soon as Mom got him back in the car at a dog show and hide it. And then he would lie on it so Mom would not take him back out of the car. He is very clever. He is already preparing me for this horrible ordeal. He would also hide his bag filled with brushes and show leads on top of the leash.

I am telling you the honest truth. You might give this a try, Gunny. Hide your dad's gun though before you leave. Besides, you are not going to have much time to go to dog shows if you are going to be my bodyguard. I need to be watched at all times.

Veni

PS: And thanks for the nice letter, Gunny. You are a great bodyguard. However, our relationship will be platonic only. Not like that movie *The Bodyguard*, I will always love you.

Letter 21a

Veni,

My dad just told me that we are moving to Sacramento next week. I will miss Carmel and the beach, but my parents are putting in a pool for me. I think you will be better off with a local boy. I hope we can remain friends and continue communicating via e-mail.

Hoover

Letter 21b

Hoover,

Oh, I will miss you. But how about Chip? An older man dog and a younger boy dog. Older? Younger? I am so confused. I have a bodyguard and a financial advisor. I will have to talk to both of them. And then there is my financial advisor, Toby. And then there is my brother, Levi. He will be tough. I do not know if he will even approve of any other dog. I can talk to him about anything however. He loves me. I just met a corgi yesterday. He is extremely handsome. And there's a younger black Lab. I have a lot to think about.

Love,
Veni

Letter 22

Hi, Mom Kristinza,

I am sorry I did not write to you, but my new mom just gave me your e-mail address. I have been so tired because my mom gave me a babysitting job with my youngest brother's son, Gage. As I mentioned to all my friends, he loves trucks and cars and insisted I play with him all day long.

After lunch, Gage does something called quiet time. Whew! My mom and I sat on the couch for about an hour or two to rest. I put my head on Mom's leg and fell asleep.

And before we knew it, he was awake again, ready for more trucks and cars. This child never sits. I had to chase him around the house or hide from him mostly. This was on Thursday at my brother Shawn's house.

On Friday, Avery went to school. She is really sweet. I wish she would have stayed home to help me. It's the same old thing: trucks, cars, and books. I am just learning English, but I was in charge of reading to Gage. He liked one book that I had to read over and over. He never got tired of it. I did. Chris, my oldest brother, came over to the house for a couple of minutes. This is when all hell broke loose. Mom could not find me. She thought I got out of the house when brother Chris left. She looked all through the house, calling my name. She looked outside and talked to several neighbors, asking if they saw me. She looked and looked and looked for about an hour. She cried. She looked again in every room, under beds, in closets, in the garage, and in cabinets. Everywhere. I was gone.

She got out the phone to call Dad but decided to look just one more time. This is when she found me. I was sound asleep, actually hiding, underneath a little table in Avery's bedroom. Mom was so glad to see me that I did not even get in trouble.

Mom took Avery and Gage to our house Friday afternoon. I was never so happy to see Levi. I was even a little happy to see Demi; however, Demi was not happy to see me. Her loss. She is still jealous of my youth and beauty. Oh well. I saw her spray bottle in the corner. She was just waiting until I fell asleep so she could spray a little bit more gray on my muzzle. I fooled her. I hid the bottle.

Gage and Avery stayed with us until Sunday. Gage, Avery's dad, brother Chris with his son, Nicholas, Cliff, and Anna came for the Super Bowl. Football? I did not understand. They yelled and screamed so much that I hid again. Mom panicked. She finally found me hiding in the corner of the garage. The kids were running, and the adults were screaming. Terrible. Next year, I hope one of my boy dog friends will take me to Hawaii.

Love and kisses,
Veni

Letter 23

Hi, Auntie,

I am five months old. The older I get, the more jobs Mom gives me. I had to babysit Gage again. As you know, Gage is my three-and-a-half-year-old nephew, my mom's grandson. He is very cute and talks very well, but he also screams and cries so loud that Mom made an appointment for me at the ear, nose, and throat doctor to check my hearing. My ears are still ringing.

Gage and Avery spent the weekend at our house with my aunt Leslie from Eugene, Oregon. Aunt Leslie is so nice, but every time she walked into the kitchen in the morning, I barked at her. Well, she scares me. She has beautiful white hair and a white nightgown. I think she is a ghost. As a matter of fact, I know she is. Then she had the nerve to tell me to be quiet. I could not help it. She is scary.

Mom promised five-year-old Avery breakfast in bed on Sunday. She was in Mom and Dad's bed. Levi and I had to carry the tray in. It was very difficult because we had to balance a glass of milk. She reminds me of Demi. She is treated like a queen. She is beautiful like Demi, but she does not stare at herself in mirror like Demi does. Thank goodness.

After the kids ate their breakfast, Mom and Dad

turned on the Disney Channel. They sat in Mom and Dad's chairs in their bedroom. They did not want to leave the movie to brush their teeth. So guess what? Dad threw out all the water in our water bowl and let them use it to spit their toothpaste. Unbelievable. After this, I jumped on Mom and Dad's bed just to get away from it all. This is when I noticed that Avery had left her milk on the end table. I drank it. I had to. There was no water.

On Saturday, Chris and Susan, my oldest brother and sister, came to our house for a barbeque with their two children, Nicholas and Ava. Guess what? Nine-year-old Nicholas won a spelling bee out of 150 children. He is going to work with me. Mom makes me study the dictionary, but Nicholas said he would help. Avery and Ava love each other, so they played and played. Nicholas helped with the kids but took over my computer. Then they ran, ran, ran, and ran. And screamed, screamed, and screamed. I had to go to Mom and Dad's bedroom and hide. I was so happy when they left.

I have news for Chip and Hoover. I am a bird dog. Last week, I took Mom a bird. I wanted her to be proud of me, so I took it into their bedroom. She had to call Dad to come home to remove it. I know she was happy, so I took her two more birds that same week. Each time, she called Dad so he could see what a good bird dog I am. I cannot understand why she had to leave the room though.

There is more, but I have to help train dogs. I will update on my boy dog friends later. I have lots to tell you.

Love and kisses,

Veni

Letter 24

My dearest Veni,

Here you will always get a *piatto di pasta*, or a pizza, for you. I see you have inherited some characteristics from your daddy. He is a super retriever, but my darling, he has never retrieved a bird. Stop doing it, please.

That's disgusting. You are a Pumi. If you are going to keep your passion for birds, please tell your mom to take you to herd geese.

Hugs,
Aunt Aurora

Letter 25

Oh, Auntie. It is so good to hear from you. I miss you. I am drooling just thinking about a pizza. I will try to be better. I cannot promise, but I will try. Are your new puppies as cute as I am? It is difficult to babysit, but I will try to be better. Hey, this is another job I could do. It is tough, but I am desperate.

Veni

Letter 26

Hi, First Mom and Auntie,

I have to find a job. And Mom might be sending me away to boot camp to find a really good dog trainer. Mom said I have destroyed too many things in the house: rugs, pillows, chairs, doggie toys, and blankets. Oh, I forgot. Their bedspread too. I thought I was doing them a favor so they could buy new, but they did not agree. Boo hoo. This is for all my girl dog and boy dog friends. Will you please talk to your parents? See below.

I can weed your garden. I promise I will learn the difference between weeds and flowers. I can dig post holes, and I can herd your sheep. I can brush your show dogs. I will even protect your home so you do not have to buy an alarm system. I bark really loud. I can chase the birds out of your yard and even retrieve them for you. I am a good retriever, maybe even better than a Lab. I will learn to go potty on the toilet so you do not have to pick up after me. And if I make a mistake, I will learn how to use the pooper-scooper. I will cook for you. One problem is that I might eat it, but I will try not to. Mom said she will send a little food, but I will have to work for my food also.

Please put in a good word for me. I do not want to

go to boot camp. Demi would be so happy. I will take minimum wage. I hear that it might go up.

Love and kisses,

Veni

PS: I am desperate.

Letter 27

Dear Hoover,

I have been such a bad girl that my mom has forgotten about boot camp. She is sending me straight to Soledog Prison. She thinks I need a twenty-four-hour guard. This prison houses the worst of the worst. This is a famous prison with famous murderers. There is a special place for dogs and, again, very bad dogs. I saw the photos of pit bulls, Dobermans, Chihuahuas, Rottweilers, a Lab, and two standard poodles. They were all in for biting people. I just bite chairs, rugs, bedspreads, pillows, Dad's slippers and sometimes Mom's, dry arrangements that are now all gone, wooden chairs, outside plants, flowers, dog beds, Mom's bathrobe after I eat everything she has in her pocket, birds, and Levi.

I do not want to go. After all, I spend a lot of time in Mom's car, and I have never chewed anything. It will be my luck that I have to share a cell with a standard poodle. Boo hoo. Boo hoo. Gunny, Lexi, Chip, Toby, and Hoover, I need your help. Perhaps send a letter to the prison on my behalf. I am, after all, a sweet, cute, and wonderful little puppy.

You can tell them how I babysat for Gage and how good I am. I had to babysit again last weekend. His mom and dad brought even more books than the last time I babysat. I read and read and read and read. I had to help with pancakes, sandwiches, and drinks. With Levi helping, I drove Avery and Gage to Target to buy new toys, and then I had to put them together when we arrived home.

Demi was in her usual queenie place on the couch. She would not help. I put Gage to bed. I was so happy. But just before, he said he had to go potty and insisted I read him a book while he sat. He picked the longest book he could find. On Sunday afternoon, I was just exhausted. Mom found me asleep in Dad's shower.

I have much more to tell you, but I have things to do. I am working on my hiding place. I will tell you about Dad's trip to Stanford and Levi's escape for three and a half hours while Mom and Dad were gone. Mom said it was the day from hell, whatever that means.

Love and kisses,
Veni

Letter 28

Oh, Veni, you are so cute. You must find a hiding place before your parents send you to prison. It looks like there are still other objects within your reach that you have left alone. I really like that orange Giants pillow. If you go to prison, can I have that pillow? In the other e-mail, Aunt Demi looks like a snooty bitch, just like my grandmother Skyye. However, Skyye tolerates me even though I pester her to no end. I hope you do not go to prison. But if you do, I understand that inmates can receive mail.

Your friend,
Willow

Letter 29

Oh, thanks so much, Willow. You can have my pillow if I go to prison. You have been a good friend, a poodle I like. Please do not tell anyone, but I have to admit that Demi and I are becoming friends. We both like to go out in the backyard and play. However, Demi still sits in one spot and stares. I think that they have to cut down on her antidepressants.

Love and kisses,
Veni

Letter 30

Dear First Mom and Aunt Aurora,
Hoover sent a letter to the warden at Soledog Dog Prison on my behalf, but Mom sent photos of what she calls the destruction from my chewing. I had to write a letter to try to save myself, so I am sending you a copy.

Veni

Dear Dog Warden, I am Veni Jackson. Hoover, my friend, sent a letter to you a few weeks ago to let you know that I really am a good puppy. But I do know that my mom also sent some photos to prove I am not a good puppy. I know I am redeemable and should not be sent to prison.

1. I sit at the door when I have to go potty. Sometimes I have to sit for ten to fifteen minutes until Mom notices. If it takes her too long, I whine until she lets me out.
2. I go right into my prison pen as soon as I see Mom put on her workout clothes. I go in without being asked. I lie down very quietly while she exercises for an hour. She exercises six days a week.
3. I babysit for Gage. He is not totally housebroken, so I have to make sure that he goes potty. I even read books to him even when he is in the bathroom. I had to sleep with Avery last Saturday because her mom forgot to send her favorite teddy bear. She cried on my shoulder for at least an hour. I told her that I would be her teddy bear and I would cuddle with her in her bed. She finally said okay, but I did not sleep all night. She would not let go of me.
4. I clean eyes: Dad's, Mom's, and Levi's. Demi will not allow it. Who would take care of this job if I were gone?
5. Levi cannot live without me, and I cannot live without him. I love him, and he loves me. Demi does not like me because I am not a poodle. This is what she holds against me. This is a heads-up just in case she writes you.

So I plead for some more time before you make a decision. I have already spent time in my jail pen, so perhaps you could consider this. Mom is talking muzzle or pulling my teeth. I think this is cruel and unusual punishment. I love her, but she believes in tough love.

There is one other thing. I am very pretty, so what if a boy dog likes me, if you know what I mean?

Sincerely,
Veni Jackson
CC: Hoover

PS: Look at me babysitting. I am watching Gage and putting away toys. What would the kids do without me? They need me.

Letter 31a

Mr. Warden
Soledog Dog Prison
Soledog, CA
April 4, 2013

Dear Mr. Warden,

I am writing on behalf of a Pumi named Veni. I have known her from the time she was a little puppy. She lives at my house. I know she sent a letter to tell you about all her attributes. I am just warning you that she stretches the truth. In fact, she lies. She is a spoiled little brat. She is the baby of the family, and truth be known, Mom and Dad think that her little antics are cute. They are not.

Each day, she destroys something new. She started chewing on a blanket chest in our family room. She will tell you that it is old and needs to be replaced. It is, in fact, very beautiful. Mom put some Chipotle Tabasco sauce on the edges of the chest. She watched Mom and then decided to lick it. No response. I prayed that her little (big) mouth would burn. The holes in the rugs are getting bigger along with Mom and Dad's bedspread.

Mom lost a black sock yesterday. Guess who had it? The toe to the sock was gone inside her stomach.

She is also nasty to me. She will not allow Levi to play with me anymore. Mom and Dad had to take me to a doggie psychiatrist, and I had to go on antidepressants. This is one bad puppy. She needs some prison time, so I am imploring you to take her. I think she needs at least three years and perhaps a new owner. Thank you for your consideration.

Demi Jackson
Champion Standard Poodle
Chualar, California

PS: Just look at this little brat. I am worn out.

Letter 31b

Dear Hoover,
Demi sent these. I really dislike her.
Veni

PS: I am sure that I will go to prison now unless Aunt Aurora gets my papers to my mom so she can get me into the show ring quickly.

Letter 32

Veni, did you really do that to your mom's rugs, or did Demi make it worse? My mom would have shot me. Veni, my sister Kristen works for San Quentin Prison, home to hardened criminals and killers. She is a counselor to the inmates, what you will be called if you are put in prison. Anyway, try to have your mom send you to San Quentin, and my sister Kristen will become your counselor and smuggle you out. I have already told her about you and have sent her your cute pictures. I think this is your only way out unless I can smuggle you away in my dad's car.

Veni, Vidi, Vici

You just need to get to your dad's office, and Harley and I will do the rest. You have a very mean sister, but then again, she is a poodle, and they are so stuck on themselves. Don't worry. We will think of something. Love you.

Your friend,

Lexi

Letter 33

Dear Mr. Warden,

I have no real proof that it was Veni, as in a photo, but I have seen it with my own eyes. Is this good enough? I know that several dynamics are going on at our house with the three children, so I am seeking some professional advice on Demi's jealousy and Veni's destructiveness, pushiness, and loudness. And then there is Levi. Levi did try to kill Veni by grabbing her leash and trying to pull her in the car. She was choking. Perhaps both Demi and Levi do not like Veni. Levi is a mommy's boy to the point of craziness.

When I get back into the car, he also tries to pull me in. He pulls on the sleeve of my coat until he gets it off. Then he takes it to the backseat so I will not get out of the car again. He even tried to pull one of my students into the car. He liked her and wanted to take her home.

I have a phone call into Cesar, the famous dog trainer, but do not discount prison time for Veni. I am a professional trainer, but a little devil is sometimes in some animals. Thanks for your consideration.

Pam Jackson
Dog Training

Letter 34

Dear Mr. Warden,

I know my mom has been waiting for a decision on my incarceration. I had a very bad day yesterday, and I am quite certain that she will be writing you, but I wanted you to hear my side of the story.

Yesterday, Demi went to the beauty shop. Levi and I went with Mom to train dogs and then picked up Demi at two o'clock. She came out of the shop looking beautiful, and she flaunted it. Many people told her what a beautiful dog she was. She had ribbons on the side of her ears and a beautiful collar and gaited to the car like a racehorse. I really dislike her.

It took us about fifty minutes to get home. I tried and tried and finally got my old collar off. I have never liked it. It is a hand-me-down after all. Demi has a beautiful collar, and so does Levi. Because I am the baby of the family and they cannot afford a new one, I got an ugly used collar. After I got it off, I chewed on it, and by the time we got home, I had managed to eat three-fourths of it. I wanted to eat the whole thing but did not have time.

I showed it to Mom when we drove into the driveway. She was really angry. She called the vet. It was now three thirty in the afternoon. She rushed me to the vet, and they took me to the back. I cried because I do not like to be away from Mom. They gave me some medicine to make me throw up. The nurse came out to tell Mom that I was throwing up a lot of stuff. About an hour later, they took Mom back to show her what was in my stomach. The ugly collar was even uglier now. There were other things in my stomach also. Tattletales. There was a tassel from a pillow.

We arrived home at five o'clock, late for us, and I had to eat some kind of canned food that is supposed to help push the rest of the stuff from my stomach. I am on this awful food for the next two days.

Mr. Warden, I think I have been punished enough. Thank you for your consideration.

Veni Jackson

PS: I am collarless. Any donations would be greatly appreciated.

Letter 35a

Dear Mr. Dog Warden,

I am Gage Jackson. I am three and a half years old. My mom, Tori Jackson, told me about your letter to Veni. Just in case you do not know, Veni is my babysitter when I go to Grammy and Grandpa's house. I have something to tell you that I think is important. She is very bossy. As a matter of fact, I do not need a babysitter in the first place. I can take care of myself.

1. When she reads me a book, I cannot understand her. She reads too fast and has some kind of weird accent. Grammy told me that she is from Hungary and spent time in Italy. I do not want to learn her language. She needs to learn mine.
2. When I walk down the long hall, she barks at me. She has a gleam in her eye. I am not a sheep. I am a little boy. I have to put my hands over my ears because she is so loud.

Levi and Demi are my favorite dogs. Could you please tell the probation officer to change babysitters if I have to have one? Thank you for your consideration.

Gage Jackson

Letter 35b

Veni, Herding abilities are only to be used on animals with four legs. Not two, you ninny. That'll get you incarcerated for sure. That dog warden can be very strict with inmates from other lands. So I suggest you tone down the bad behavior just a little. That possibly will result in you just being on probation instead of lockdown, which I do not think you would like one bit. Bread and water twice a day. No boy dogs. No apples. No hedges. You had better think about this very seriously, Veni. Prison record stays with you the rest of your doggone life.

Mollie

Letter 36

Hi, Gage,

My name is Hoover. I am a three-year-old Lab. I know why Veni is so bossy. I was a student of your grammy. She is the master of bossy. She wanted to be in control all the time. I was only one at the time. She put me on a down-stay for five minutes and hid in the bushes to scare me. One time, she told me to come, and at the same time, she threw a chain and hit me in the rear end. Gage, stick with Veni. It could be worse. You might have Grammy babysit you the next time.

Hoover

Letter 37

Dear Veni,

After much thought and several meetings with my colleagues, we have made a decision. We feel that incarceration might be detrimental in your case. We have concluded that military school is the way to go. This is only after you finish high school with excellent grades. We know you are a very bright girl, but you have many behavioral problems, which tells us that you need major discipline vis-à-vis the military.

We have also decided not to punish your mother. She has trained and owned several dogs, all of which have been good dogs. Only you, Veni. We realize that sometimes an owner can get a bad apple. Perhaps you ate too many of them. One other thing. No boy dog friends. You are too boy crazy.

We have assigned you a probation officer. You have to check in every Thursday at 10:00 a.m. Do not be late.

Mr. Warden
Soledog Dog Prison
Soledog, California

Letter 38

To all my dear dog friends,

Oh no. I just received a letter from the warden at Soledog Dog Prison. I am going to try to be a better girl, but I do not know how I will ever give up my boy dog friends. I just can't.

I just met a new boy in Oregon. He is black and handsome. His name is Bad Boy Jack. Hoover is yellow, Chip is brown, and the old gentlemen Striker is yellow. Jack is a black Lab who actually has a job. He loves me, like all my boy dog friends. And he can afford diamonds.

I find myself very attracted to Labs; however, I am still young, eight months old now, and I know I will meet more boy dogs. I am going to have to be very sneaky. I am good at this. Jack is very tall and very smart; however, his dad Robert said I was a better retriever. Only because I love boys to chase me.

Tears,
Veni

PS: I think I will consider the navy. I am a good swimmer and a good retriever. My goal is the Navy Seals. I love adventure. But how will I ever be able to live without Mom? Boo hoo.

Letter 39

Dear First Mom and Auntie,

My mom took me for my first meeting with my parole officer at Soledog Prison. He told me that I was one lucky little puppy. The warden made his decision at the last minute, he said. This was only after he saw my photo. I guess that this is when good looks make a difference. He thought I was too beautiful and felt one of the really bad dogs might take advantage of me. I saw my mom smirk out of the corner of my eye.

My mom said to me that Demi's photo next to bitch is starting to dim, and my photo is taking her place. She said I am the boss with Demi and Levi. I make them toe the line. Just because I bark in Levi's ear down the hall every day. Just because his hearing is getting worse. Mom even took him to the ear, nose, and throat doctor. Just because Demi waits to run to the bedroom after I get there. So this makes me a bad girl? They need to toughen up.

Next week, my parole officer is going to take me into the doggie jail. He wants me to see what almost happened to me. He told me not to wear anything revealing. No lipstick and no makeup. I asked if Levi could go with me, and he told me no. Levi did not chew the rugs, bedspread, and hundred-year-old boxes. I did.

Veni, Vidi, Vici

Wish me luck. I am scared. However, Mom thinks I can take care of myself. She feels that all the bad dogs might be afraid of me.

Love and kisses,
Veni

Letter 40a

Dear family and friends,

You all know that I have not written for quite awhile. There was a good reason. I was kidnapped. My friend Hoover warned me that I should be careful because of the many photos that Mom sent to her friends. Kids were being found from photos on the Internet and kidnapped. And it happened to me.

Mom went into her favorite yogurt shop in the Crossroads in Carmel. She always leaves the windows down for Levi and me. A man came to the window on my side and offered me an apple. Levi told me no. But I could not help myself. Our apple tree has not had apples for six months. I was starving for an apple. He gave me a bite and then grabbed me and drug me out of the window. Levi barked, growled, and yelled for Mom. When Mom came out, I was gone.

There were two men. They threw me in the backseat of their car and took off. I heard them say that they finally got the most beautiful Pumi for breeding. They had several at their shack in Denver, but none as pretty as I was. They also said that I had beauty and brains. I cried. I laid in the backseat for hours and hours.

They finally stopped to get something to eat. They

put me in a trunk. I had to get out, so I started chewing and chewing. I chewed right through the trunk because I have had plenty of practice and jumped out. I ran and ran. I had no idea where I was. I ran through bushes and water. Thank goodness. I was so thirsty. And I ran through traffic. The cars were zooming by so quickly. I was in Arizona. I saw a sign that said "Welcome to Arizona." It was hot.

Several people tried to catch me, but I outran them. They all wanted me. Finally, I had to lie down to rest. I fell sound asleep. When I woke up, I was in a big truck. The driver was very kind, but I was leery. I would not talk to him. He gave me some food left over from the truck stop: chicken fried steak, gravy, and mashed potatoes. I wanted to refuse, but I finally gave in. Nothing except apples has tasted so good.

He asked where I lived, and I told him some place in California in the country. He got on his cell phone and found out my name was Veni Jackson. There was an Amber Alert for me. And he knew my dad. His truck hauled produce. I fell asleep.

The next thing I knew, I was home. Mom and Dad had balloons, new dog toys, and, yes, a big apple. All my family and friends were there to greet me. But I did get grounded and was told in no uncertain terms to never ever take apples from a stranger.

Love and kisses,
Veni

Letter 40b

Dearest Veni,

Hmm, I am seeing shades of the Garden of Eden here. The apple, remember? I think we need to go back to the basics, dear. Ah, how quickly temptation overtakes you. More lessons for Veni. Fret not. You will get it in time.

I am seeing that you somewhat like the corner of drama. Good guess, eh? And if I were you, you may take some time to unwrap Demi and Levi's coalition. It sounds like they have something going and you aren't a part of it. Do you think that maybe it could be your behavior? Wait. That is way too much in a short time to absorb, but give it some thought. Sleep on it. Maybe you will get the answer in your dreams. You have the brains, and I know you will use them. It is for the best.

Always with love,
Aunt Jude

Letter 41

Dear friends,

Because I was kidnapped not too long ago, I had a visit from the FBI. They have been looking for me for a long time, but I was in Aunt Aurora's name until a couple of months ago. I had no idea who the FBI was, but Mom explained that they are the Federal Bureau of Investigation. They wanted to talk to me. They came in a uniform and wore badges. I barked at them, ran into Mom and Dad's bedroom, and hid under the bed. I do not like uniforms.

They talked to my mom about my friend, Vladimir, that I met in Hungary when I was five months old. My first human mom introduced us. He is a Russian wolfhound from Russia. The FBI thinks I am a spy and passing information from the United States to my friend Vladimir in Russia. What next?

My mom and dad made me go to the family room to talk to the two men. One was very nice to me; the other was not too nice. They questioned me for four to five hours. I was exhausted. I told them over and over that we just talked about food, chewing, digging, chasing birds, and how much I love apples and dislike Demi. Vladimir was my boyfriend from the time I was a little puppy. He loves me, and I love him like a brother now. I have met many other handsome boys, but Vladimir still considers me his girlfriend. It has actually been a problem. I tried to explain this to the FBI, but they did not believe me.

They finally left but said I cannot take any trips. My trip to Italy has to be put on hold. They said they would be watching me. Well, guess what, Mr. FBI? I can smell you first, so I will be on my best behavior at all times. Vladimir, stop e-mailing and writing me. Our relationship is over. I love you as a friend only.

Veni

Letter 42

Hi, Veni,

I think you need to get out of the country ASAP. My dad owns a printing company. He could get you another airline ticket under a different name. If you could send me a recent photo, he could also make you a passport. Do not trust the FBI. They work for the government, and he has read all your mother's e-mails. I will miss you, but you must go.

Hoover

Letter 43

Hi, Hoover,

My life has changed forever. I really liked it before, except for Demi, because I got to play with Levi and go with Mom to watch her train dogs. Trouble is, she is now training me for competition and even taking me to dog shows. I do not like it. And I do not like strangers looking at my teeth and touching my body. It is none of their business. Mom is so disappointed in me. Sorry, Mom. She even took me to another trainer to get another opinion of my problem. I thought she is a trainer.

The trainer had me do strange things, like go over PVC pipes with hot dogs in between them. Mom did not quite understand the theory for this. I kind of liked it until I stepped on a pipe. It moved and frightened me, so I did not want to do it anymore. I was inside a weird building that was attached to a car wash. Mom is desperate, I guess.

Another trainer online suggested that Mom not show me in competition for a year. Now, I liked this trainer. But then she suggested that I go to rally classes, herding, fly ball, or agility. Mom is busy trying to find a good trainer for all these. Come on, Mom. Just let me be a dog.

Mom had a very bad morning this Sunday. Levi and I wanted her to get up at four o'clock. Dad always gets up at this time except on Sunday. Dad is out of town, so we started licking Mom's face, playing, and barking. Then Levi lay on top of her. I could see that she was having trouble breathing. She told us to go back to sleep. We did for a while until Dad called at five o'clock.

We stared at her because she was talking on the phone. Yes. Time to get up. Mom told us to settle and go back to sleep. She was just nodding off again when Levi saw the horses and jumped off the bed, barking. And I followed. The trouble is that I stepped right on Mom's eye. She yelled at me. I think she has a black eye.

Then Levi started throwing up, so she jumped out of bed, looking out of one eye, and started cleaning. She noticed that toilet paper filled the whole bedroom and sitting room. Well, I get a little bored in the middle of the night. So we got punished. Sorry, perfect Demi.

Mom cleaned the bedroom, scrubbed the windows, fed the cats and horses, emptied the dishwasher, cleaned the family room, and finally fed us. Our other punishment was grooming and giving us a bath today. She told us that we had better not wake up at four o'clock next Sunday morning. I miss all my dog friends.

Love and kisses,
Veni

Letter 44

To all my loyal friends,

I told you I had much to say. Last night, Mom and Dad left us home. I hated every minute of this. They still put me in a crate because they do not trust me. Levi and perfect Demi got to stay free in Mom's and Dad's bedroom. Sometimes I do not like either one of them.

They had dinner with my two sisters, Tori and Susan; my two brothers, Chris and Shawn; and, of course, the grandkids, Nicholas, Gage, Avery, and Ava. It was a big celebration. My sister Tori was sick for a while. Tori is so brave and never complained, as I would. She is my idol because she was never afraid, like me, and had a positive attitude. I have to rethink dog shows. Maybe I need to go to her training school.

Today, brother Shawn came to visit. Avery and Gage came with him. Avery had to ride Buttercup, her horse. She really wanted to stay in the house because Mom spoils them, but Shawn made her ride. She had a good time, and so did Mom. She got to spoil her grandkids. I tried to keep them in line, but Mom got on me. Levi licked them, and so did Demi and me a little, but not too much. I think they like me because I am so cute though.

I was so worn out by the time they left. It is difficult

being a dog. I am a herding breed, so I have to watch them all the time.

Love and kisses,
Veni

Letter 45

Dear friends,

I have so much to tell you. Mom took me to two shows that she had already entered. So instead of listening to the advice of two other trainers, she decided to do her own thing. She showed me in competition. Perhaps she should have listened. Mom told the first judge that she was working on my problem, so she was very kind. She took her time going over my body, and I was better. I actually thought I should have won, even though my tail was straight out instead of down.

The next day, I did not show as well. Come on, Mom. You were not supposed to show me at all. Even though I was a bad girl, I had so many people say I was the cutest dog they had ever seen. Of course, I already knew this. There was one dog at the show that I did not like. Mom was very upset with me, but come on, Mom. It was only one. And she did not like me either. So, guess what? She entered me at three more shows. She thinks I need the experience. I think she is not a good listener.

I think I forgot to tell you about Levi. He was a very bad boy. As you all know, we have two horses. Levi, much to Mom's chagrin, barks as we leave the house every day. Mom gets out the can. She told him to be quiet. It was actually another word that I had never heard. And he listened. In fact, he was so quiet that she was puzzled. She looked in the backseat while she was driving, and we were not there. Then she noticed that the back window was open. Levi had put his paw on the electric window. Both of us were gone. She panicked.

She could hear Levi barking, so she looked in the horse paddock, and there was Levi, chasing the horses. He jumped the fence. I cannot jump like Levi, but I was chasing them outside the fence. Levi came when he was called, but I was more resistant. Let's face it. Levi is a mommy's boy. Levi jumped back over the fence when she called him. I, on the other hand, was enjoying my independence. She may have to find another trainer. Levi and I got mud all over the inside of Mom's car. Demi was her favorite dog that day. Perfect Demi.

Love and kisses,
Veni

Letter 46

Dear dog friends,

Well, today I tried and tried to get Levi to breed me, but he will not. I begged and begged. I cried and whined, but to no avail. He finally growled at me. Mom had to take Levi to Dad's office because she said I was driving poor Levi crazy. She thought it would be the other way around, but she said she was not surprised. Because it is me, Veni. Mom said I am a hussy. She is thinking jail time would be good.

I am so frustrated.

Love,
Veni

Letter 47a

Hi, friends and fans,

Levi finally decided that he was interested in me. I am so happy. It is about time. Mom and Dad would not leave us together this morning. Dad took Levi to work because we were both driving them crazy. I was so depressed when he left. It was just Mom and me. She had to tell me that she is not a dog, if you know what I mean?

Love and kisses,
Veni

Letter 47b

Hi, my friends,

Mom should have been watching. She was unloading groceries from her car when she heard a cry in the backyard. When she looked out, she saw something that I still do not understand. She opened the door to let in Levi and me, and we came in with our rears stuck together. It did not take long for us to get unstuck, but Levi was hurting. But not me. I kept going after him. He was having a difficult time walking and was sore. He wanted nothing to do with me. He actually growled. He has not been near me since. It is not fair. I still love him. I actually love boy dogs.

Mom is very happy today because we are both quiet. Whew. She is hoping that this is all over. She told Dad that it has been hell. She signed me up for some dog shows again. I wish I would stay in season for a year.

Love,
Veni

PS: Levi is neutered.

Letter 48

Dear friends and fans,

Mom told me to wish everyone a happy Thanksgiving. She said it has something to do with Pilgrims and Native American Indians. I do not know anything about this because I am from Hungary. She said that most everyone cooks a turkey on Thanksgiving Day. In my opinion, the turkeys are probably not too thankful. I feel sorry for them. Run, turkeys. Run.

My mom took me to a horse vet yesterday. I am a dog,

not a horse. She has been worried because I have not been eating. They entice me with hamburger, cheddar cheese, treats, and really good canned food, but I walk away, come back, and eat a couple of bites. It takes me twenty to thirty minutes to eat. I am just not hungry. The horse vet and two assistants threw me on my back, held my neck until I could hardly breathe, spread my little legs, and took a picture. They then put some cold stuff on my stomach and took more pictures. Then to add insult to injury, they took blood from my neck. It took them forever.

The vet tried first and could not do it, so she gave the job to her assistant who finally took my blood. How dare they! I was so scared. Levi was with me, and he tried to protect me, but Mom told him no. Mom was so happy because the vet said I was okay, except I think I am pregnant. How does she know what I think? I did not like her very much.

When we left, Levi jumped in the car first and grabbed my leash to pull me in. It is very nice of him, but he almost choked me. My neck was already sore from the vet trying to strangle me and poking at my neck. Not a good day.

Love and kisses,
Veni

PS: Mom and Dad are leaving us tomorrow for nine days. Boo hoo. They decided not to leave us alone this time. They decided to splurge for a good dog sitter. I wonder if she eats turkey. I hope Mom and Dad can come up with the money to pay her. They still have all those old things in our house. I worry.

Letter 49

Hi, friends and fans,

I am grounded. As you know, Mom and Dad went on vacation for ten days. They said they had a great time visiting all our relatives, but they left us at home. We love our dog sitter, Amanda, but Levi and I miss Mom and Dad so much when they leave. Demi, the beautiful poodle, says that we are crybabies. She is a champion after all and tells us to be more independent like her. It is Levi that should be grounded because he tried to jump the fence, even with that horrible collar that shocks him, because he wanted to find Mom and Dad. He also made a big mess in the family room. He had a little problem. He had some smelly stuff on his rear end that he got on the couch and many other places in the family room. Amanda, as sweet as she is, was a little upset because she had to clean the couch and put Levi in the dog tub to wash him off. I, on the other hand, was a good girl. I ate well, even though I am still convinced that I am going to have puppies, and I was nice to Demi.

Because I missed Mom so much, I will not leave her alone. I cannot help myself. I stare at her and bark. I grab her bathrobe. I bark at her when she is on the computer. The computer is mine. And yesterday morning while she was still in bed at five o'clock, I jumped on the bed and started nipping her and whining. I wanted her to get up.

Dad gets up at four o'clock, feeds us, and then takes us back in the bedroom. I bark all the way down the hall. I want Mom awake. This morning, I tried a new thing. I grabbed her nightgown and tried to drag her out of bed. I whined a little also. She grounded me.

I just do not think it is right that they leave us at home. Maybe they will think about it the next time they leave. But Mom said that a real vacation is when she does not have to put up with me. Well!

Love,
Veni

PS: By the way, I am as pretty, if not prettier, than Demi.

Letter 50a

Dear Auntie Aurora,

I am really in trouble this morning. Mom was covered up to her neck with a blanket, so at five o'clock, I did not have any choice but to grab her hair with my teeth. She says she does not have much hair to begin with and needs all she has. All my privileges have been taken away. My toys are locked in the safe. I have been so good about not chewing rugs but may not have a choice now. I am still waiting for a ticket to Italy or Hungary to see my real mom and my auntie. Mom is talking about boot camp and Soledog Dog Prison again. Christmas is coming, Auntie Aurora.

Love,
Veni

Letter 50b

Dear Veni,

Oh, don't worry so about the whispers of Soledog. I hear that the climate is lovely there and they do have a great rehabilitation program for the incorrigibles. Only get nervous if Mom mentions Gitmo. By the way, Christmas is coming soon. Better clean up the act for a while.

Your cousin,
Jude

Letter 51

To all my friends,

This is my second Christmas in the United States. Over my first Christmas, I could hardly understand what my new parents were trying to tell me. I had to study the dictionary. Here are the words I hear and understand the most. No, Veni. No bark, Veni. Oh no! Look what you chewed, Veni. Drop it, Veni. Veni, stop it. This is when I grab Mom's bathrobe with my teeth. I gave it a new look. I like it.

It has been quite a year. I was kidnapped. I had to go to competition classes and dog shows. I hated it. I became a woman. I terrorize Levi. He loves it. And I continue to drive Demi absolutely crazy. It is a good thing that she is on antidepressants. Her vet is considering Valium just because of me.

I babysat for Avery and Gage many times in 2012. It was a tough job. All that reading. Mom said reading is good for me. I think that Dad and Mom should do the reading. After all, Levi and I had to make breakfast and then put it on a tray so Avery and Gage could have breakfast in bed on Sunday mornings. Do you think they are a little spoiled? And then, they did not even share so I had to help myself.

I changed after I became a woman. Dad gets up at four o'clock and feeds us, but I really feel that Mom needs to get up at the same time. I try something different every morning to get her out of bed. This morning and yesterday, I whined and whined in her ear. She would not get up, so I pulled the covers off her. You know what she said? "Stop it, Veni." When she goes into the kitchen every morning to clean and eat, I bark at her when I feel it is time to go back to the bedroom. You know what she says. "Veni, no bark." She needs to be on my schedule.

Mom is making cookies for Nicholas, Ava, Avery, and Gage. It is going to be a tough week because she will be in the kitchen for hours. I know I will have to whine, pull on her bathrobe, and tell her to hurry up. And then, she never offers me a cookie. On a good note, I did find an apple yesterday. I took it in the house and jumped up on the bed to show it to Mom. She did take a photo because she thinks I am so cute. I am.

I hope that all of you have a wonderful holiday. I get to go to both my brothers' houses for Christmas Eve and Christmas Day. Mom and Dad do not trust me at home alone. I do not get it, but I am glad because I get to go with them and Levi and Demi have to stay at home. I do feel sorry for Levi.

Love and kisses,
Veni

Letter 52

Dear friends,

I mentioned that Levi and I had to babysit for Avery and Gage the day after Christmas. We picked them up at six thirty in the morning. Gage and Avery got new bikes for Christmas, so many of their new toys from Santa came with them.

Mom had to train a dog on Friday. So many dogs misbehave. So handsome Leopold babysat. Gage wanted to ride his new bike, which made Leopold very nervous, especially after Mom pointed out that Gage is a little accident prone. It happened. Gage ran his bike into the front gate, fell off, and cried. He wanted his Mommy. Leopold was so nervous because Gage did not want his help. I am not sure if Leopold will ever have children after his experience with Gage.

Avery always comes into our bedroom at five in the morning. She is a little nervous because Demi and Levi make such a ruckus. I, on the other hand, am quiet. She got into bed, and I licked her face, but then I started nipping at her. She was lying on my puppies. As you know, I became a woman. Mom said I went through a false pregnancy. It was not false. I had puppies on the bed. This was why I whined and tried to pull Mom out of bed. I pulled her nightgown, hair, and blanket. Avery did not want to come into our bedroom until she heard us go down the hallway to get fed in the morning. I am better now that all my puppies were sold. I do miss them, but they were a lot of work.

Avery and Gage stayed with us for four days. Then they went back to stay with Tori's mom, Jan, from Monday until Friday. We got them back for the weekend, just when we were starting to catch up on some sleep. Mom got sick, and she was in bed all day on Monday after the kids left. Levi and I stayed with her. We had to take care of her now: breakfast, lunch, and dinner. We do almost all the cooking now, but we are not allowed to bake cookies.

Love,
Veni

PS: Did you hear that cannabis—or pot—is now legal in Colorado. I hear Mom is going to take a trip to Colorado and promises dog cookies just for me. I knew I was special.

Letter 53

Dear Hoover,

My mom is trying her best to change me or kill me. She took me to Gilroy, California, to a very mean trainer who grabbed my leash and hooked me up far away from my mom. She left me there all by myself while she and Mom talked. I struggled and struggled to get loose, but I could not move. My legs got wrapped up in my leash, so Mom started to go over to help me, but the mean trainer would not let her. My photo faded under the word "bitch" in the dictionary, and her photo is bright and clear. The enclosed area not only had a hook for me but a big table with a chain and hook. It looked like a guillotine. I was praying that she would not hang me.

But soon, she came over, unhooked me, and put me on the guillotine table. Oh no! She stacked me and then had her daughter try to give me a treat. I would not take it. I am sure it had poison in it. She told me that I had nice angles, whatever that means. She was trying to be nice, but I knew better. She really wanted to hang me. Has Mom lost her touch with dogs? She signed me up for a class with that mean trainer to build my confidence. I am going to have a headache every Monday night.

To add insult to injury, Mom took me to herding class in the same week. All kinds of dogs were there. A trainer by the name of Clint tried to take me into an enclosure with two sheep. I ran back to Mom. So she had to go in with me. I chased the sheep. I can run really fast. The sheep ran from me, but Clint had a big, long stick to keep me from getting too close. I did not like that stick. I went in three times that day. I was so tired all the way home.

The next week, Mom took me back. I am getting the hang of it a little better now, but I found out that it is a very dangerous sport. Clint put in some faster sheep the second time I went in. I was chasing a sheep, and the sheep ran right into Mom. She fell on her rear end. I felt sorry for her, so I went over to apologize. She had goat poop all over her rear mixed with sheep poop. This was when I discovered how delicious sheep poop is. Yum yum! Forget chasing sheep. It is as good as an apple.

Mom leaves for Hawaii in two days. I want to go too, but she will not let me. She says she needs a break from me. My dad will be in charge of all of us. Dad and I had a plan. He let me in the closet yesterday morning while Mom was in bed. When she got up, she could not find one of the shoes she had out to wear on the plane. I chewed it. Dad and I are grounded.

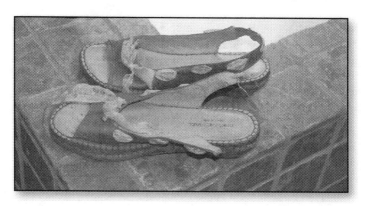

Love,
Veni

Letter 54

To all Veni's friends,

As you know, Veni is my sister. I know you are all friends of hers, except perhaps for Harley. I am writing because Veni has some serious problems. My mom took me to the nose, ear, and throat doctor and found out that I do have hearing loss. Veni barks in my ear every morning as we are all running down the hall for breakfast. My mom would use the can, but my dad is very silent. He is not a disciplinarian.

As you also know, Mom exercises six days a week. I

know when it is time for cool down, as does Veni, but she does not care. She thinks Mom should stop when Veni wants her to stop. She stares at her and barks. Her bark starts off sounding like a cough and then gets louder when Mom keeps exercising. Mom tells her to be quiet, but she does not listen. I love her, but she needs a tough trainer.

And another thing, Veni has several balls. She does not like to share. But when I get the ball, she stares at me, runs to Mom, and barks. She is a tattletale. I finally just give it up so she stops her barking. I am sick of it. Take the ball, Veni, and stuff it. Come on. There are several balls.

Here is the new thing. She takes the ball to Mom, drops it, and barks. She wants her to throw it for her. Then if it rolls under something, she runs to Mom again and barks. I watched this morning. Even if the ball does not go under something, she stares at the spot, looks at Mom, and barks. I see Mom getting down on her hands and knees to find it, and nothing is there. She gives Veni a look of disgust, but I see a gleam in Veni's eyes.

One last thing. Veni goes to herding and obedience classes. She loves to tell me about it. She says, "I bet you would love to herd sheep." I noticed she does not say anything about obedience class.

Mom took us in to a doctor to check our IQ. We both have a high IQ, but on the devious scale, Veni excelled. She was a perfect ten.

Thanks for listening.

Levi

Letter 55

To all my friends,

I do not know where to start. I must say that I will have to tell you about Leopold, a twenty-year-old German friend of my mom and dad. He is so handsome that Demi could not keep her eyes off him. She flirted and flirted to the point that it was really disgusting. I, on the other hand, was more ladylike. I thought he was handsome too, but I thought discretion was the better part of valor. Demi needs to go to school to learn how to be a lady.

Levi did not like him. He was jealous. I know I was

Leopold's favorite, even though Demi was glued to him at all times. He petted her, but his eyes were on me the whole time.

Christmas Eve at Chris and Susan's did not start out well at all, even though I had Leopold all to myself. Mom got me out of the car on a leash, and that very instant, the neighbor's Australian cattle dog ran over to bite me. Mom hid me behind her and yelled at the top of her lungs. NO! The dog went home, but he is known in the neighborhood to charge people and other dogs. I was so scared. Mom kept me on leash in the house so I did not get into the cookies. Rude! Especially after I was almost killed. All the kids loved me. Again, who wouldn't? And, Demi, I got to sit in the backseat with Leopold. Ha!

Christmas Day at Shawn and Tori's was much better. There were no mean dogs, and I was allowed off leash. Dinner looked delicious, even though I was not allowed any again. We did not stay too long because Shawn and Tori were leaving for Viet Nam the next day. This is another story because Levi and I had to babysit early the next day. And, Demi, Leopold was all mine again on Christmas Day. Sorry. Not really.

On Christmas 2013, I was almost killed. I was offered no cookies, turkey or ham, mashed potatoes and gravy, and handmade rolls. But there was Leopold and time away from beautiful Demi.

Love,
Veni

Letter 56a

To my dear friends,

I saved this for last. I was kidnapped again in 2013. But this time, I was kidnapped by some small, weird-looking people with big heads. I was on Mom's bed when she was sick and fast asleep. They came through the skylight above Mom and Dad's bed and scooped me up. It was so quick that Levi did not even bark or try to help me. He acted like he was paralyzed.

I flew in the sky to a round aircraft. They were very nice to me, but they said they had to do some testing. I asked them why. They told me that they had heard about me and I was so unique that they wanted to test my brain. I told them no and I wanted to go home. They told me to relax. All of a sudden, I was home and back in bed. My head hurt. Levi acted like I had never left, and Mom did not wake up.

Mom and Dad did not believe me until they saw it on the news. Mom would like to know what they found out about my brain so she can train accordingly. She said I have been a challenge.

Love,
Veni

Letter 56b

Read below.

To all that it may concern, We studied Veni Jackson in Chualar, California, in the month of December 2013. We wanted to alert her Mom and Dad of our findings because we think they are quite significant and feel she definitely needs help from a professional dog psychiatrist.

Extreme mischievousness filled her frontal lobe. She feels she is the most important dog in the family. She also thinks that she is better than any other dog ... period. She has a jealous streak, especially of girl dogs. She knows she is cute but wants to be beautiful like her sister Demi. She would like to find a job so she can have a little face-lift. She looks forward to chewing, barking, whining, picking on Levi, and making trouble for her Mom and Dad with great abandon. She plain does not care. She thinks only of herself.

Our suggestion: a little shock treatment to her brain. It may take more than one.

Good luck,
Alien Ship #556000

Letter 57

To all my friends,

Mom went to Hawaii to help her good friend (and my youngest brother's mother-in-law) to decorate her condo. I tried to sneak into Mom's big suitcase, but not one inch was left for me. I wonder if she wore all those clothes. She could have left a few items home so there would be room for me. We all went with Dad to take her to the airport in San Francisco. I could not stop crying. Levi took it like a man, and Demi sneered at me and called me a baby. Ugh! Sometimes I cannot stand her.

Sunday was our first day without Mom. Dad tried to make up for our loss by feeding us more and giving us snacks. Monday and the rest of the week, we all went to Dad's office. Two Yorkies—Lexi and Harley—go to work there also. Harley is a little—and I mean little—monster. He runs around the big desk that everyone in the office shares. He barks, and he shakes. Then he runs to his food bowl. He will not share. It became my job to put him in his place. So I did. After all, I was trying to take care of my dad because, a few months ago, Harley pooped on one of his orders on his desk. Dad was not happy. Everyone else in the office laughed. Like Dad, I did not think it was funny.

Levi got in trouble on Tuesday. He jumped the fence at Dad's office to chase the horses. Dad yelled at him to come back, but when he didn't, he yelled, "Cookie!" That did it. He got a pretzel. I am sure he was a little disappointed.

Finally, Saturday came, and Dad surprised us by loading us into Mom's car to pick up Mom in San Francisco. I rode in the front seat so I could lie on Mom's pillow. It smelled like her. I was so excited. We sat there for a long time waiting to see her. Then all of a sudden, we saw her walking toward the car. Levi and I jumped into the front seat of the car when we saw her. We were so excited that she could not even get in the car. We were kissing her and wagging our tails, and I whined. Demi is such the lady. She was staying in the backseat, but Mom gave her a big kiss anyway. Why?

I told my mom that I would try to be a better girl so she would not have to take anymore trips. She told me that I had a lot to prove before she could believe me.

Love,

Veni

PS: Mom said I have to go on a diet. I loved all that extra food that Dad gave us.

Letter 58

Hi, all!

I got in big trouble a few days ago, and I mean big trouble. And it is all Demi's fault. Mom took all three of us to the Crossroads last Tuesday. Demi usually goes to the office with Dad to sell produce, but it was her grooming day. She had on her beautiful collar. I am still wearing a hand-me-down. And yes, I am jealous. Mom got her out of the car to take her to the groomer, and I could not help myself. I jumped out of the window. I have never jumped out the car window before, but I wanted to be beautiful too. Mom cannot afford to take Levi and me to the groomer. She puts us in an old tub in the garage and washes us herself. Demi is the privileged one just because she is a champion and struts like a racehorse. Ugh!

Mom saw me running toward her. The car saw me too, but I knew that. And she screamed, "Veni, come!" I came back and jumped in the car, but I think I almost gave Mom a heart attack. Mom told Dad that her heart was racing. I saw the car. Mom rolled the windows all the way up. It is a good thing it was cool, but I think she was trying to suffocate me.

My punishment was boot camp video exercise with Jillian Michaels called "Biggest Loser." I do it with Mom. She ordered me doggie weights. I heard Mom call Jillian the b-word, but I concur now. Her photo is the biggest in the dictionary by the b-word besides mine. Mine is fading. However, Mom does not agree.

Love,
Veni

PS: I will tell you about Clint, my boyfriend, later.

Letter 59

Dear Hoover, Willow, Lexi, Gunny, Bad Boy Jack, Cracky, and all the rest of my dog friends,

It is midnight on Saturday night, and I could not sleep. I snuck out of bed to turn on the computer while Mom and Dad were sleeping. I needed to talk. Mom took me to herding class on Saturday morning, and I was so excited that I kept jumping in the front seat about fifteen minutes before we even arrived. I saw Clint, and I pulled my mom over to him. I missed him so much. He took me in to herd goats with my mom twice that day. It was Mom's birthday weekend, so she had to leave early. I did not want to go. I pulled Mom again so I could sit by my Clint. I sat right in heel position next to his leg.

My mom told me that we had to go, but I did not want to leave his side. She took me to the car, but I would not get in. She had to lift me in.

On the way home, I pouted. My mom usually had the news on, but her XM radio was not working. I was so happy. I know she wants me to learn all about politics, but to be honest, I've had enough. I know who our president is, including all the congressmen and woman, governors, and so forth. So she turned on music instead. I was so happy. I needed to relax and think about Clint. I think I am in love. Sigh. Is it okay to be in love with a human?

There was a love song on the radio called Endless Love. It made me think about my love Clint all the way home.

Now, how do I get rid of his wife and dogs? I know his wife will be jealous because I am a cutie, or so they say. He can keep one of his border collies because she ignores me, so I know I will be the boss. I need some advice.

Love,
Veni

Dear most exotic and beautiful Veni,

It's perfectly normal to have a first crush. It happens all the time. My first crush was on my mom. What a beauty!

My advice is to try to see Clint as a mentor or dear uncle and not a boyfriend. More appropriate for a boyfriend would be a dog, like, for instance, me. Woof! There are different kinds of love in the world, and you'll learn about the romantic kind soon enough. Clint is not—I repeat not—a good candidate for a husband. You mentioned his wife and other dogs. Ya, that's a deal breaker right there.

You don't want the word "bitch" defined in the canine Webster's with your picture.

Other things you don't know about Clint might help you work through this. He's a total Raiders sports nut. I think he may go to lots of games, and they don't let dogs into the stadiums. So where does that leave you? Home moping on the couch?

Clint doesn't actually own all those sheep. I just learned this. They belong to Michele. So my advice is to be very nice to her. Put your paw on her lap and stuff like that. And check out Clint's dogs. I've never met his wife, but his dog Bet is super loyal and skilled at her work. Clint will never leave her, even for you. Though, remember that I'm always here. Woof!

All that aside, Clint is also my favorite person in the world, almost like a god really. He has access to so many sheep. I love his voice. The only voice I don't like is the one that forms the words "Ranger, no." And I don't like it when he pokes that stick in my shoulder when he thinks I'm too close to his sheep. Other than that, he's pretty much my favorite human.

So thank you for sharing. I understand your feelings for Clint. Good luck with sorting them out. If I can ever be of service to you, as a friend, let me know. Just a friend though, because, sadly, I'm neutered.

I hope this biscuit of dog wisdom is helpful.

Ranger, the corgi

Letter 60

To all my dear friends,

Last weekend was so exciting. I got to go to herding practice with Mom, and most importantly, I got to see Clint. Mom took me in three times to chase—I mean, herd—goats. I am getting to know them personally now. Some I like, and some I don't. I saw one give me a dirty look. Mom told Clint, who was standing outside the gate, that I was not working very well for her. Truth be known, I wanted Clint. The second time Mom took me in, I did the same thing on purpose. Clint finally came in with me, and I was so excited that I did really well. Mom said a cuss word. Not nice, Mom. Clint had a little talk with Mom about what she had to do to keep me more up. I can solve the problem, Mom. Just send me in with my boyfriend, Clint.

I do not get to see him this weekend because Mom and Dad have a graduation party in the afternoon. I am depressed. The girl, Mom and Dad's friend's daughter, is now a doctor of psychiatry. I think they are going to talk to her about Demi. Not me, of course. I am a good girl. And maybe Levi. He is a true mommy's boy.

Mom has about had it with Levi and me. Every morning when we leave the house to train dogs, Levi starts jumping from the backseat, toy in mouth, barking and barking at the horses, cats, and squirrels. As you might recall, he opened the window of the car and jumped out. He is so annoying that I get in the front seat on Mom's lap so I do not have to listen to him. Mom gets really mad at me because I turn on the seat warmers, the hazard lights, and the four-wheel drive. It is Levi's fault.

This morning, she decided to turn on the music really loud, and the song that came on was "Good-bye, Norma Jean" about a beautiful actress named Marilyn Monroe. Levi knew who she was because Mom's father loved her. And Dad has pictures in his office, thanks to Grandpa. Levi, you can have Marilyn, but I have Clint.

Love,
Veni

Letter 61a

To all my friends,

As you know, I have a hand-me-down collar that I hate. Levi and Demi have beautiful collars, but Mom and Dad, as I told you before, cannot afford to get me a new one. Well, guess what? I got a new collar. Demi and Levi wanted to give me an early birthday surprise, so they got on Dad's computer and checked on Amazon because Demi knows his password. And they ordered a new collar for me. Today, they had me open my birthday present, and there was a brand-new collar. I have to admit that it is not very good looking, but I said nothing because it was so thoughtful. I did not think that Demi would even think about my birthday.

Levi and Demi put it on me and told me to go look in the mirror. I could not see it very well, but I was so happy and thanked and thanked them. We left Mom and Dad's bedroom to go to the kitchen. I love to bark all the way down the hall. I barked, and something strange happened. I thought Demi nipped me, so I licked her face and went on my back to apologize for whatever I did to cause her to nip me. I tried barking again, and the same thing happened. What did I do to Demi?

I have not barked for the last two hours now. I knew it

was too good to be true that Demi thought about me. She gave me a strange collar. And how about my best friend Levi? I feel so alone.

Veni

Letter 61b

I love that little Veni, but I have hearing loss from all her barking. And, Gage, we were thinking about you too. After all, you have to cover your ears every time you come to visit us. And Demi still has a smile on her face.

Levi

Letter 62

To all Veni's friends,

We are in deep trouble. Mom and Dad are making us do community service. We have to scrub all the cells for those poor dogs at the SPCA for two months. We also have to walk. They refuse to drive us.

Mom noticed that Veni was so quiet yesterday and looked confused and depressed. She could not understand why until she noticed a new collar. She asked Veni where she got the new collar. Veni told her that it was her birthday present from Demi and me and it felt weird every time she barked, so she stopped barking. Mom took it off immediately and then sat Demi and me down to talk.

First of all, we are grounded from ever using the computer, and we are especially in trouble for using Dad's Amazon account. Besides community service at the SPCA, we are in charge of feeding the horses. We are not allowed to chase them. And we are to feed the cats. This, we feel, is cruel and unusual punishment. How will it be possible not to chase the cats? If we do, we will be punished for the rest of our lives, they say.

Veni's new collar is put away forever for her. Mom and Dad were thrilled to hear her bark this morning. This is what Veni is all about. She loves to talk. I guess my hearing will get even worse, and Mom, what about Gage?

Talk about depressed.

Levi and Demi

Levi is going to wear the collar today in the car. Let's see how he feels when he starts barking at the horses.

Mom

Letter 63

Dear Lexie,

I trust that my letter will be shown to your mom and dad. Do say hi to Harley, even though I am not his favorite dog. I am sure that you know why I am writing. I had to take care of my mom last night after she arrived home from your home. I put ice on her neck and aloe vera on her forehead. She was in a bad way. She still looks like a big Mack truck hit her today.

After much thought, I have decided that I am going to call my brother Chris to see if he can recommend a good personal injury attorney. I looked in the doggie yellow pages, but the closest dog that does personal injury is in San Jose, California. You see, even though she drank a beer, it was not really enough beer to fall up your steps. There should only be one step. I feel, from what she described, that the designer of your house, not your parents maybe, should be sued. After all, my dad fell on those same stairs about ten minutes after they arrived. Mom thinks that everyone must think that they had a lot to drink before that arrived for the party. They did not. Those steps are dangerous, and I think they do not like the Jackson family. Perhaps they need an exorcism from a priest.

I am going to recommend that they not sue for much.

Mom and Dad are not greedy. I am thinking around a quarter million. Mom is in bad need of a new car. And I could use a little money myself. I have to replace two rugs, two chairs, a couch, and a bedspread.

I love you, Lexi, so I hope you will not be mad at me, but I must take care of my parents. We need the name of your contractor, if you do not mind looking it up for me. I would greatly appreciate it.

Love,
Veni

Letter 64

To all my friends,

Just to let you know so you can spread the word even though I will be advertising in the yellow pages and Facebook, I am starting Veni's Dating Service. I will require all dogs to give me full disclosure of their jobs, personality flaws, illegal activities like stealing food from garbage cans, and so forth. And I will not accept felons. I saw too many of them when I had to visit Soledog Prison. They are very scary.

They will have to fill out a form with many questions. I will find out everything about them. It is going to be just for dinner for fine whining and dining. You can trust me to find "just the right" doggie for you. I am a herding breed, so I do not miss anything. I am a very good judge of character. And boy, dogs will be required to pay. The cheap boy dogs will be flushed out right away.

My charge will be three hundred dollars for my service. And I will provide the caterer in case there are any wedding bells. My dad is a good cook and knows exactly what dogs like.

Veni, Vidi, Vici

Please send résumés to Veni Jackson via Mom's e-mail. I am working on my own e-mail address.

Thank you,
Veni Jackson

PS: I do have many things in our house to replace, and besides, I might find a good-looking boy dog for me. Clint is married.

Letter 65

Hey, Veni,

It's me, Champion Gunny. I would love to sign up for your dating service. I have huge ribbons to show all the ladies. I think my parents can afford your service too. You see, I got my championship in four days so I didn't cost them much. I know they are looking for someone for me to be happily ever after with. Please post my profile to your pupbook:

- Breed: Pomeranian
- Sex: Only with my stuffed toys
- Name: Gunny Stop Barking
- Likes: Girl of all breeds
- Dislikes: Other studs

Champion show dog looking for the future Mrs. to share beautiful walks with while I sniff you. Must love my humans despite their annoying nagging about leg lifting. Will provide a beautiful home and all the future offspring one could ever want.

Call me, Veni.

Gunny

Letter 66

Oh, Gunny, my first customer. Thank you. I will find a beautiful girl for you. Maybe me? But I think you might be too short, although you are very handsome. I have to think about it, but in the meantime, I will send this out to some girl dogs, so we will see what happens. I will keep you informed.

Veni

PS: Mom is mad at me because I do not have one point for my championship yet.

Letter 67

Veni,

My mommy told me about you and your new venture, so here is my profile. My name is Shilo, and yes, my parents named me after the Neil Diamond song. I know that it's a really corny, old song, but what can I say? It's my parents' generation, so forgive them. I love them anyway.

My mommy told me my heritage is purebred Coton De Tulear female from Madagascar. I will be three years old in September. I love to play all day long and have been told that I'm very cute but can be a little handful at times. I heard Daddy say to Mommy that it's okay. It gives me a little personality. I have been to school, and most of the time, I do pretty well. I am, after all, still two. I would be interested in meeting someone that likes to play and have fun. And he needs to be very brave because he would need to meet my parents first. Mommy is not a problem as long as you are nice, but Daddy said he would have to talk with the boy. And that would be a good time to clean the gun before I could meet anyone. Daddy has never talked like that before, and I'm not sure what a gun is. And I don't know what he wants to talk about. Mommy says there is a protocol to follow, and this would be a big girl thing to do.

Good luck in your new venture,
Shilo

Letter 68

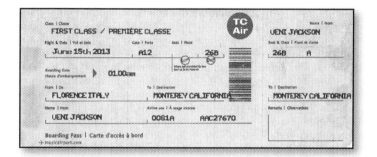

Dear Hoover,

My dad got a card in the mail today. You know it was his seventieth birthday. Didn't I tell you they were old? He just loved it. I have never seen him so happy. He was laughing, laughing, and screaming. Yes, yes, yes. He had tears in his eyes. They were happy tears.

Demi, Levi, and I were just staring at him in pure wonder. He finally showed it to Mom. It was a one-way ticket for me, first class to Florence, Italy. One way. It was from your dad. It was really nice of him to think of me, but how am I going to get home? Does he not want me to come home? Perhaps this is his way of getting rid of me? The more I think about it, this is his plan. Huh.

Well, I will go. I will have some pasta, garlic bread, and red wine. I will enjoy myself at Aunt Aurora's house;

chew a few things, starting with their beautiful rugs; dig up some plants; bark my little head off; boss all the other dogs around; and circle Aurora's boyfriend and quickly give him a little nip on his leg. I will see you SOON.

Chow.

Love and kisses,
Veni

PS: Hoover, I really think you should look for another home. My sister's mother is in charge of Lab rescue.

Letter 69

Dear Hoover,

I am writing you because I trust you. I had to tell someone what I did, so I thought it was best to tell you. Please do not tell another human or animal. I could go to jail or Soledog Prison for sure. But I had to get this off my chest.

Just before Mom went to Arizona, she took me to see Clint for herding. Mom told him that she could not make the next Saturday because she would be out of town. I pouted. Clint looked at me and saw how sad I was, so he said to Mom, "Well, Veni knows the way."

I thought about what Clint said, so I talked to Levi and Demi. I did not want to talk to Demi, but I had to. I knew she was tall enough to drive. She did not want to do it, but I told her that I would do all her chores for a week. She finally gave in, but of course, she had a sour look on her face. We all got up early and waited for Dad to go to work. We had to do this very early because it was imperative that we got home before Dad. We got up at the crack of dawn and took off with Demi behind the wheel. I gave her directions, and she put them in Mom's GPS system. I hate to admit this, but poodles are smart. I wanted to listen to "Endless Love" because it reminds me of my Clint, but Levi wanted to listen to "Good-bye,

Norma Jean" because he is in love with Marilyn Monroe. Levi and I had a fight.

Demi said, "If you kids do not stop fighting, I am going to turn this car around and take you home."

I gave her a look to kill, but shut my mouth because I had to see Clint.

We arrived in Hollister, California, right on time. I ran right to Clint, but Levi wanted to see the sheep and goats too. I told him no, but he ran over and jumped the fence to chase my goats. It took Clint twenty minutes to catch him. Clint finally had to throw a net over Levi to capture him. This is the only day that Demi was my favorite dog. Levi took all my time with Clint.

It was time to leave. I did not even speak to Levi on the way home. Demi asked me if I were hungry because she found some money in Mom's car. I really was not too hungry because I was so upset with Levi. But when Demi pulled into the drive-thru at McDonald's, the hamburgers smelled so good. She got French fries also because she thinks she is French. I wolfed down my hamburger and Levi's. Serves him right.

Well, this is the end of my story. I would not even look at Levi for more than a week. He tried everything to make up, but I put my paw straight up in the air and told him not to talk to me.

Love,
Veni

PS: While Mom was gone, I learned how to jump the fence. I was so proud. I heard a car in our driveway and thought Mom was finally home, so I wanted to see her.

I really like doing it now so I can chase cats. Levi has to wear a certain collar because he jumps the fence also. Mom put a throw can on top of the gate to see if this is going to work. She showed it to me and rattled it. I hate that can. If it does not work, I get to wear a new collar. At least I will finally get a collar. 'Bout time.

Letter 70

To all my loved ones—boo hoo! The United States government stole my e-mail about Demi, Levi, and I driving to Hollister, California, to see Clint and my goats. Why are we so important to them? The government cannot even find some very important e-mails of their own, but they sure can find mine. Boo hoo. I think I might be better off in Hungary or Italy. Their government would never do this. The United States is a strange place.

An officer of the law came to our house to arrest Demi, Levi, and me. He told us that we were driving without a license. Demi should have been the one in trouble, but because it was my idea and Levi went along with it, all three of us had to go to the doggie courthouse. He put us in handcuffs to take us away to court. The doggie judge, a Rottweiler, growled, scolded, and growled some more. He told us that we were bad doggies and deserved jail time.

I said, "But I am in love with my teacher and just had to go see him."

And he said, "No excuses, please, Miss Veni Jackson. And do not speak unless I ask you to speak."

What a jerk.

They had to select a jury of all different dog breeds. Our trial was set for June 27, 2014. I wanted my brother Chris to represent us in court, but they would only accept dog attorneys. Our attorney was a basset hound. He could hardly walk around the courthouse and did not speak very well. He was court appointed because we had no money. Mom and Dad are poor, as you know. Let's face it. He did a lousy job. We were found guilty. They sentenced us to six months in county jail.

I wanted to write because I only have a few minutes before they take us off to our cells. You will not be hearing from me for quite some time. They will not permit me to have a computer, and I can only talk on the phone for two minutes a day. My new doggie dating service will have to be put on hold also.

I will miss all my friends. I just wanted to tell you that I love you. Please say some doggie prayers for us. We do not know whom we will meet in jail. I am sure there are some hardened criminals. It is a good thing that all three of us watched Mom do her kickboxing. It may come in handy.

I hope that Demi, Levi, and I will see you again.

Love,
Veni

And the last thing heard was the clanging of two cell doors. One for Demi and Levi together and one for Veni all alone. She was, after all, the instigator.

Letter 71

Dear Veni,

I will miss you while you are in jail. So sad to find out that you are incarcerated. Demi and Levi too? Wow. I will bet that your parents are drinking a toast with champagne now that they have the house to themselves. At least you will not have to go to dog shows anymore. I have heard that they can be worse than prison. Keep the faith. Maybe Clint will visit you.

Your friend,
Willow

Characters in This Book

1. Levi, Veni's Pumi brother
2. Demi, Veni's standard poodle sister
3. Aunt Aurora, the owner of Veni's father from Italy
4. Hoover, her yellow Lab friend
5. Toby, a terrier
6. Willow, a standard poodle friend
7. Chip, her chocolate Lab friend
8. Chesty and Gunny, Pomeranian brothers
9. Cracky, a mixed-breed shorthair pointer
10. Kristinza, Veni's first mom from Hungary
11. Lexi, Veni's Yorkie friend
12. Mollie, a miniature Aussie
13. Bad Boy Jack, a black Lab from Oregon

Printed in the United States
By Bookmasters